This Book Belongs To:

Illustrated by Simon Scales

Type Design by Mark Vincent

Produced by Hanover Group, Inc.

Design consultation and Production coordination:
Georgopoulos Design Associates

Publisher's Publication Data
Levine, Lauren F.

First Edition
Summary: In rhyming style, the children and animal friends of Grayla, the cat, solve the mystery of her broken meow.
[1. Juvenile literature – Fiction. 2. Laughter – Fiction. 3. Stories in rhyme. 4. Cats – Fiction.
5. Farm yard animals – Fiction. 6. Friendship.] I. Scales, Simon, ill. II. Title

ISBN 978-0-615-18185-1

To order additional copies of this book, visit
www.thebrokenmeow.com

Printed in Singapore

Dedicated to
Barry Smith
Matt Hanover
Peaches and Night-Night

www.thebrokenmeow.com

In the blue barn
And the purple corral
Live the **animal friends**
Of Lizzie and Cal

Bathing in sun
Near the corral
Sat **Grayla** the cat
With her **charming meow**

1

"Let's visit Grayla
Our **green** eyed cat
She is **soft**, she is **sweet**
She's a little bit fat"

2

This cat who loves
To **purr** and **meow**
Looked up at Lizzie
And mewed

"Iggy -Howl!"

"Iggy-Howl?" said Lizzie
A word **never** before
Heard from their cat
They **had** to know more

The dog overheard
This **broken meow**
And knew that the kids
Were expecting **bow-wow**

Wagging her tail
Instead of bow-wow
The big, fuzzy dog
Barked a loyal

4

"**Splish-Pow!**" said Lizzie

"I don't know how

But it **sounds** like our dog

Has **sprained** her **bow-wow**"

The chickens that **peck**
And gobble and cluck,
Stared at the cat
And then blurted,

"Hip-Huck!!"

"The chick's cluck is stuck!
Let's check on the cow"
They hoped for **moo**
As a greeting somehow

The cow looked up
And instead of a **moo**
She **twinkled** at Grayla
And snorted,

"She's **stubbed** her **moo!**"
Said Lizzie to Cal
We better run, **quick**
And check the corral"

In the corral
The horse looked their way
She swallowed her oats
And then **burped,**

"Furple-Snay!!"

"It sounds like our horse
Is **missing** her neigh
Let's check on the pig
I'll show you the way"

They **ran** to the barn
To listen for **oink**
But the big, pink pig
Squealed,

"Bipsy-Kerbloink!!"

"The pig **pulled** her **oink!**
Like the horse and the cow
We need some **help**
We need it **now!**"

14

They picked up the phone
And called **Dr. Rick**
He comes right over
When the animals are **sick**

"Dr. Rick our cat
Has a **broken meow**
Our big, fuzzy dog
Has **sprained** her bow-wow"

15

"Our chick's **cluck** is stuck
Our cow **stubbed** her moo
Something is wrong
What can we **do?**"

"And then there's the horse
Who's **missing** her neigh
The pig **pulled** her oink
Oh what a day!"

16

Dr. Rick came quick

And he knew right away
The **culprit** was Grayla
He had this to say

"She's used up her sounds
Since she talks all the time
She **meows**, she **purrs**,
She **chirps** and she **whines**"

"Her animal friends
They took a vow
To make silly sounds
Since she **broke** her **meow**"

19

"Let everyone rest
For a week and a day
Make sure they are quiet
Then we'll see what they say"

VET

BARN

Dr. Rick came back
After they had a rest
"Let's hear all of your sounds
Give it your best"

Dr. Rick looked around
While Lizzie and Cal
Watched their animal friends
As the pig squealed,

The horse nickered, **"cluck"**

The cow mooed, **"meow"**

The cat howled, **"oink"**

The kids cried, **"WOW!"**

«cluck

«moo

The chicks clucked a **"moo"**
The dog woofed a **"neigh"**
"Dr. Rick," asked Lizzie
"Will our friends be **okay?"**

"oink"

"meow"

"moo"

"wow!"

"neigh"

24

"They have traded their sounds"
Laughed Dr. Rick
"They are **playing** with us
They're **not** really sick"

Grayla gave a green wink
To the bright **Dr. Rick**
Grinning at the kids
She was no longer **sick**

She **purred** at the horse
Who was eating some hay
And after a snort
Out nickered a,

"Neigh!!"

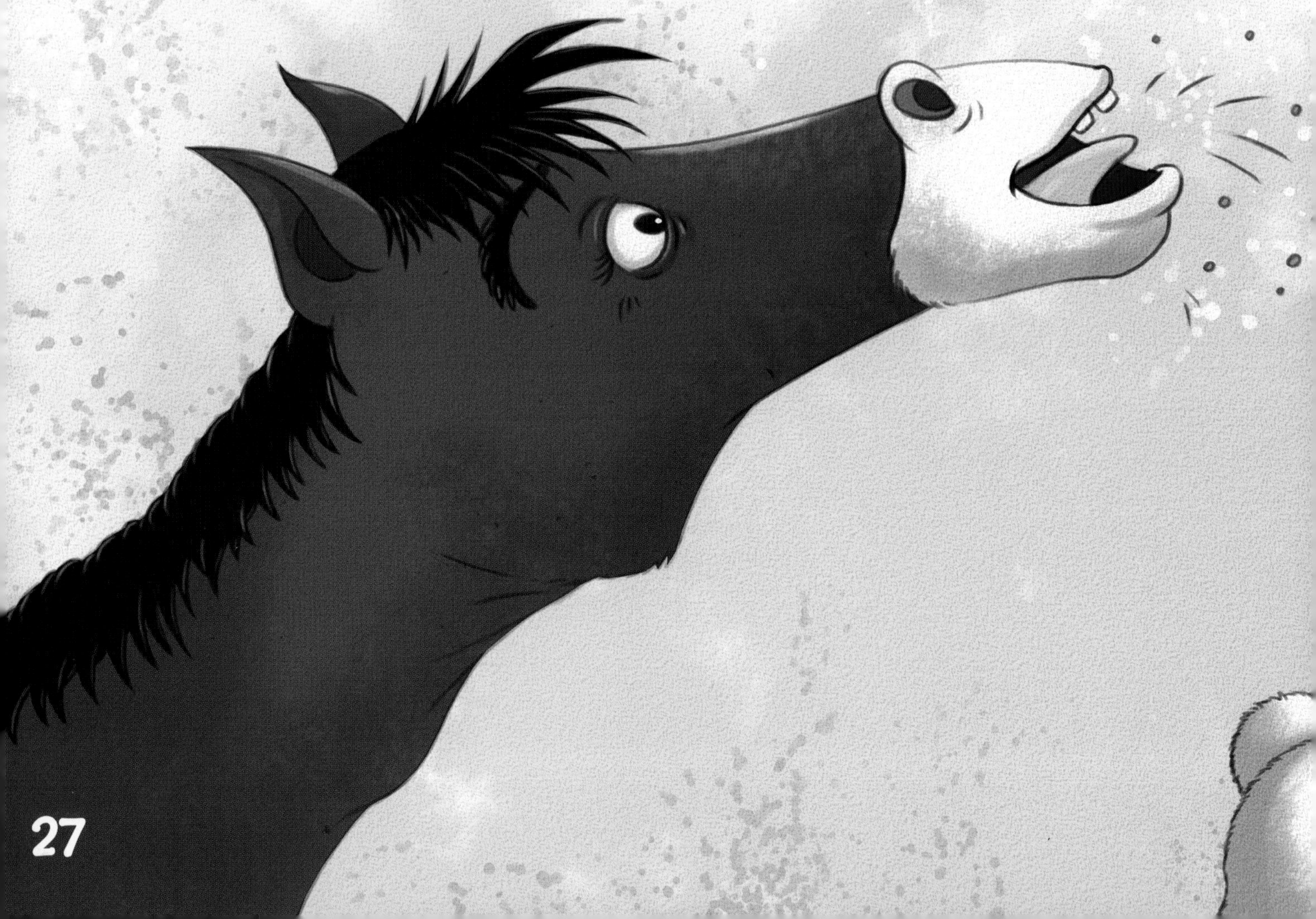

The pig squealed an **"oink"**

The dog woofed **"bow-wow"**

The chicks cheeped a **"cluck"**

The cat smiled **"meow"**

All that was left
Was the cow and her **moo**
They waited to hear
What she would do

"bow-wow"

"meow"

"oink"

"cluck"

And **all** gave a cheer
Dr. Rick and the kids
Drew the animals near

"**Thanks Dr. Rick!**"

"Let's go home for the night
Grayla **fixed** her **meow**
And everyone's alright"

Dr. Rick said, "**goodnight**"
And "goodnight," said Cal
But **instead** of goodnight
Lizzie whispered

"Meow"

33